Dear Parents,

Welcome to the Scholastic Reader series. We have taken over 80 years of experience with teachers, parents, and children and put it into a program that is designed to match your child's interests and skills.

Level 1—Short sentences and stories made up of words kids can sound out using their phonics skills and words that are important to remember.

Level 2—Longer sentences and stories with words kids need to know and new "big" words that they will want to know.

Level 3—From sentences to paragraphs to longer stories, these books have large "chunks" of texts and are made up of a rich vocabulary.

Level 4—First chapter books with more words and fewer pictures.

It is important that children learn to read well enough to succeed in school and beyond. Here are ideas for reading this book with your child:

- Look at the book together. Encourage your child to read the title and make a prediction about the story.
- Read the book together. Encourage your child to sound out words when appropriate. When your child struggles, you can help by providing the word.
- Encourage your child to retell the story. This is a great way to check for comprehension.
- Have your child take the fluency test on the last page to check progress.

Scholastic Readers are designed to support your child's efforts to learn how to read at every age and every stage. Enjoy helping your child learn to read and love to read.

—**Francie Alexander**
Chief Education Officer
Scholastic Education

For Peter and his cousin Dan
—J.M.

For Jack Griffin
—W.W.

ISBN 0-439-68054-9

Text copyright © 2004 by Jean Marzollo.
"Arts & Crafts" from *I Spy* © 1992 by Walter Wick; "Carnival Warehouse" from *I Spy Fun House* © 1993 by Walter Wick; "Masquerade" from *I Spy Mystery* © 1993 by Walter Wick; "Monster Workshop" and "Sand Castle" from *I Spy Fantasy* © 1994 by Walter Wick; "Storybook Theater" from *I Spy School Days* © 1995 by Walter Wick; "A Blazing Fire," "The Fountain," and "Ghost of the Night" from *I Spy Spooky Night* © 1996 by Walter Wick.

10 9 8 7 6   06 07 08
Printed in the U.S.A. 23
First printing, October 2004

I SPY

A SCARY MONSTER

Riddles by Jean Marzollo
Photographs by Walter Wick

Scholastic Reader — Level 1

SCHOLASTIC INC.
Cartwheel BOOKS®

New York   Toronto   London   Auckland   Sydney
Mexico City   New Delhi   Hong Kong   Buenos Aires

I spy

 two paint jars,

snaky blue hair,

 two horns,

 a ruler,

 and a little black bear.

I spy

a skeleton,

 a set for tea,

 two fish,

a ship,

and a leaf from a tree.

I spy

a witch,

a fancy chair,

a monster tree,

and orange hair.

I spy

a crossbow,

a shield white and red,

 two small flags,

and a sand-dragon's head.

I spy

a black cat,

 a green crocodile,

a ladder,

a pail,

and a lion's smile.

I spy

a tiger,

two D's,

three O's,

a colorful pencil,

and T-Rex's toes.

I spy

a red eye,

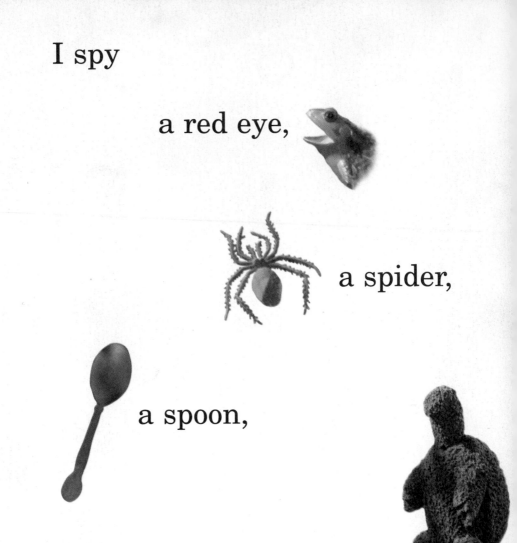

a spider,

a spoon,

a spooky turtle monster,

and a bright full moon.

I spy

a paintbrush,

two yellow laces,

a little green gear,

and five toothy faces.

I spy

a cork,

 a shoe that's blue,

  two bears,

two dogs,

 and a pudgy pig, too.

I spy

a fork,

a dinosaur,

 an E,

a frog,

and a ghost that's looking at me!

I spy two matching words.

two paint jars

a set for tea

two dogs

I spy two matching words.

a ship

little green gear

 little black bear

I spy two words that start
with the letter M.

spooky
turtle monster

orange hair

 bright full moon

I spy two words that start with the letters CR.

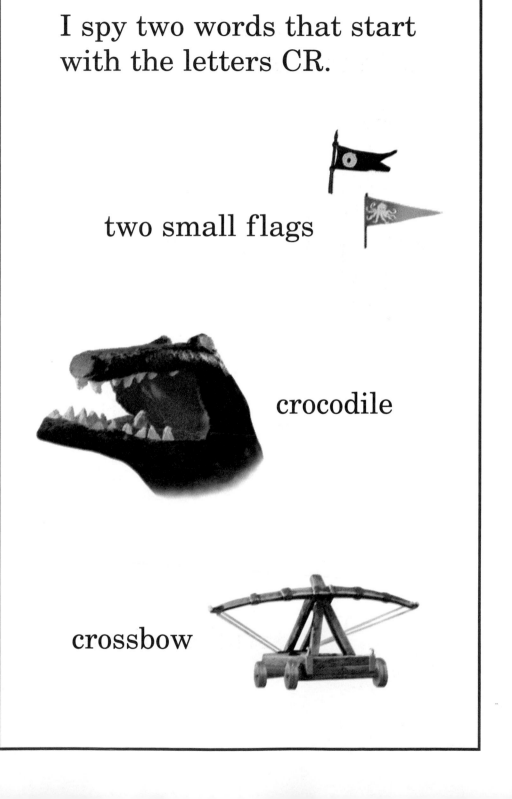

two small flags

crocodile

crossbow

I spy two words that end with a silent letter E.

a toothy face

 a ladder

lion's smile

I spy two words that end with the letters SH.

pail

two fish

paintbrush

I spy two words that rhyme.

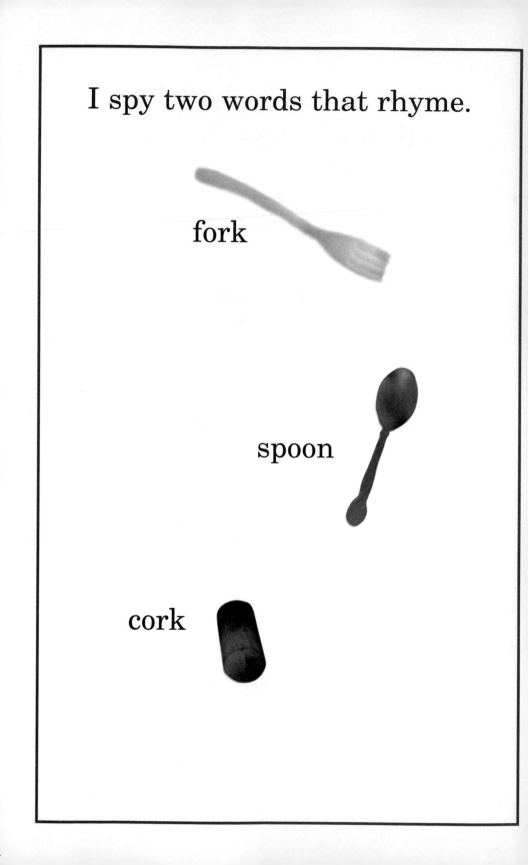

fork

spoon

cork

I spy two words that rhyme.

a dinosaur

shield white and red

bright full moon

Fluency Fun

The words in each list below end in the same sounds.
Read the words in a list.
Read them again.
Read them faster.
Try to read all 12 words in one minute.

moon	**mail**	**air**
noon	**nail**	**fair**
soon	**pail**	**hair**
spoon	**tail**	**chair**

Look for these words in the story.

blue	**little**	**two**
eye	**from**	

Note to Parents:

According to *A Dictionary of Reading and Related Terms*, fluency is "the ability to read smoothly, easily, and readily with freedom from word-recognition problems." Fluency is necessary for good comprehension and enjoyable reading. The activities on this page include a speed drill and a sight-recognition drill. Speed drills build fluency because they help students rapidly recognize common syllables and spelling patterns in words, and they're fun! Sight-recognition drills help students smoothly and accurately recognize words. Practice these activities with your child to help him or her become a fluent reader.

—**Wiley Blevins,**
Reading Specialist